The Feud Buster, and
The Haunted Mountain

Robert E. Howard

The Feud Buster, and The Haunted Mountain

By

Robert E. Howard

The Feud Buster

These here derned lies which is being circulated around is making me sick and tired. If this slander don't stop I'm liable to lose my temper, and anybody in the Humbolts can tell you when I loses my temper the effect on the population is wuss'n fire, earthquake, and cyclone.

First-off, it's a lie that I rode a hundred miles to mix into a feud which wasn't none of my business. I never heard of the Hopkins-Barlow war before I come in the Mezquital country. I hear tell the Barlows is talking about suing me for destroying their property. Well, they ought to build their cabins solider if they don't want 'em tore down. And they're all liars when they says the Hopkinses hired me to exterminate 'em at five dollars a sculp. I don't believe even a Hopkins would pay five dollars for one of their mangy sculps. Anyway, I don't fight for hire for nobody. And the Hopkinses needn't bellyache about me turning on 'em and trying to massacre the entire clan. All I wanted to do was kind of disable 'em so they couldn't interfere with my business. And my business, from first to last, was defending the family honor. If I had to wipe up the earth with a couple of feuding clans whilst so doing, I can't help it. Folks which is particular of their hides ought to stay out of the way of tornadoes, wild bulls, devastating torrents, and a insulted Elkins.

But it was Uncle Jeppard Grimes' fault to begin with, like it generally is. Dern near all the calamities which takes places in southern Nevada can be traced back to that old lobo. He's got a ingrown disposition and a natural talent for pestering his feller man. Specially his relatives.

I was setting in a saloon in War Paint, enjoying a friendly game of kyards with a horse-thief and three train-robbers, when Uncle Jeppard come in and spied me, and he come over and scowled down on me like I was the missing lynx or something. Purty soon he says, just as I was all sot to make a killing, he says: "How can you set there so free and keerless, with four ace-kyards into yore hand, when yore family name is bein' besmirched?"

I flang down my hand in annoyance, and said: "Now look what you done! What you mean blattin' out information of sech a private nature? What you talkin' about, anyhow?"

"Well," he says, "durin' the three months you been away from home roisterin' and wastin' yore substance in riotous livin'—"

"I been down on Wild River punchin' cows at thirty a month!" I said fiercely. "I ain't squandered nothin' nowheres. Shut up and tell me whatever yo're a-talkin' about."

"Well," says he, "whilst you been gone young Dick Jackson of Chawed Ear has been courtin' yore sister Ellen, and the family's been expectin' 'em to set the day, any time. But now I hear he's been braggin' all over Chawed Ear about how he done jilted her. Air you goin' to set there and let yore sister become the laughin' stock of the country? When I was a young man—"

"When you was a young man Dan'l Boone warn't whelped yet!" I bellered, so mad I included him and everybody else in my irritation. They ain't nothing upsets me like injustice done to some of my close kin. "Git out of my way! I'm headin' for Chawed Ear—what *you* grinnin' at, you spotted hyener?" This last was addressed to the horse-thief in which I seemed to detect signs of amusement.

"I warn't grinnin'," he said.

"So I'm a liar, I reckon!" I said. I felt a impulse to shatter a demi-john over his head, which I done, and he fell under a table hollering bloody murder, and all the fellers drinking at the bar abandoned their licker and stampeded for the street hollering: "Take cover, boys! Breckinridge Elkins is on the rampage!"

So I kicked all the slats out of the bar to relieve my feelings, and stormed out of the saloon and forked Cap'n Kidd. Even he seen it was no time to take liberties with me—he didn't pitch but seven jumps—then he settled down to a dead run, and we headed for Chawed Ear.

EVERYTHING KIND OF floated in a red haze all the way, but them folks which claims I tried to murder 'em in cold blood on the road between War Paint and Chawed Ear is just narrer-minded and super-sensitive. The reason I shot everybody's hats off that I met was just to kind of ca'm my nerves, because I was afraid if I didn't cool off some by the time I hit Chawed Ear I might hurt somebody. I am that mild-mannered and retiring by nature that I wouldn't willing hurt man, beast, nor Injun unless maddened beyond endurance.

That's why I acted with so much self-possession and dignity when I got to Chawed Ear and entered the saloon where Dick Jackson generally hung out.

"Where's Dick Jackson?" I said, and everybody must of been nervous, because when I boomed out they all jumped and looked around, and the bartender dropped a glass and turned pale.

"Well," I hollered, beginning to lose patience. "Where is the coyote?"

"G—gimme time, will ya?" stuttered the bar-keep. "I—uh—he—uh—"

"So you evades the question, hey?" I said, kicking the foot-rail loose. "Friend of his'n, hey? Tryin' to pertect him, hey?" I was so overcome by this perfidy that I lunged for him and he ducked down behind the bar and I crashed into it bodily with all my lunge and weight, and it collapsed on top of him, and all the customers run out of the saloon hollering, "Help, murder, Elkins is killin' the bartender!"

This feller stuck his head up from amongst the ruins of the bar and begged: "For God's sake, lemme alone! Jackson headed south for the Mezquital Mountains yesterday."

I throwed down the chair I was fixing to bust all the ceiling lamps with, and run out and jumped on Cap'n Kidd and headed south, whilst behind me folks emerged from their cyclone cellars and sent a rider up in the hills to tell the sheriff and his deputies they could come on back now.

I knowed where the Mezquitals was, though I hadn't never been there. I crossed the Californy line about sundown, and shortly after dark I seen Mezquital Peak looming ahead of me. Having ca'med down somewhat, I decided to stop and rest Cap'n Kidd. He warn't tired, because that horse has got alligator blood in his veins, but I knowed I might have to trail Jackson clean to The Angels, and they warn't no use in running Cap'n Kidd's laigs off on the first lap of the chase.

It warn't a very thickly settled country I'd come into, very mountainous and thick timbered, but purty soon I come to a cabin beside the trail and I pulled up and hollered, "Hello!"

The candle inside was instantly blowed out, and somebody pushed a rifle barrel through the winder and bawled: "Who be you?"

"I'm Breckinridge Elkins from Bear Creek, Nevada," I said. "I'd like to stay all night, and git some feed for my horse."

"Stand still," warned the voice. "We can see you agin the stars, and they's four rifle-guns a-kiverin' you."

"Well, make up yore minds," I said, because I could hear 'em discussing me. I reckon they thought they was whispering. One of 'em said: "Aw, he can't be a Barlow. Ain't none of 'em that big." T'other'n said: "Well, maybe he's a derned gun-fighter they've sent for to help 'em out. Old Jake's nephew's been up in Nevady."

"Le's let him in," said a third. "We can mighty quick tell what he is."

So one of 'em come out and 'lowed it would be all right for me to stay the night, and he showed me a corral to put Cap'n Kidd in, and hauled out some hay for him.

"We got to be keerful," he said. "We got lots of enemies in these hills."

We went into the cabin, and they lit the candle again, and sot some corn pone and sow-belly and beans on the table and a jug of corn licker. They was four men, and they said their names was Hopkins — Jim, Bill, Joe, and Joshua, and they was brothers. I'd always heard tell the Mezquital country was famed for big men, but these fellers wasn't so big — not much over six foot high apiece. On Bear Creek they'd been considered kind of puny and undersized.

They warn't very talkative. Mostly they sot with their rifles acrost their knees and looked at me without no expression onto their faces, but that didn't stop me from eating a hearty supper, and would of et a lot more only the grub give out; and I hoped they had more licker somewheres else because I was purty dry. When I turned up the jug to take a snort of it was brim-full, but before I'd more'n dampened my gullet the dern thing was plumb empty.

When I got through I went over and sot down on a raw-hide bottomed chair in front of the fire-place where they was a small fire going, though they warn't really no need for it, and they said: "What's yore business, stranger?"

"Well," I said, not knowing I was going to get the surprize of my life, "I'm lookin' for a feller named Dick Jackson —"

By golly, the words wasn't clean out of my mouth when they was four men onto my neck like catamounts!

"He's a spy!" they hollered. "He's a cussed Barlow! Shoot him! Stab him! Hit him in the head!"

All of which they was endeavoring to do with such passion they was getting in each other's way, and it was only his over-eagerness which caused Jim to miss me with his bowie and sink it into the table instead, but Joshua busted a chair over my head and Bill would of shot me if I hadn't jerked back my head so he just singed my eyebrows. This lack of hospitality so irritated me that I riz up amongst 'em like a b'ar with a pack of wolves hanging onto him, and commenced committing mayhem on my hosts, because I seen right off they was critters which couldn't be persuaded to respect a guest no other way.

WELL, THE DUST OF BATTLE hadn't settled, the casualities was groaning all over the place, and I was just re-lighting the candle when I heard a horse galloping down the trail from the south. I wheeled and drawed my guns as it stopped before the cabin. But I didn't shoot, because the next instant they was a bare-footed gal standing in the door. When she seen the rooins she let out a screech like a catamount.

"You've kilt 'em!" she screamed. "You murderer!"

"Aw, I ain't neither," I said. "They ain't hurt much—just a few cracked ribs, and dislocated shoulders and busted laigs and sech-like trifles. Joshua's ear'll grow back on all right, if you take a few stitches into it."

"You cussed Barlow!" she squalled, jumping up and down with the hystericals. "I'll kill you! You damned Barlow!"

"I ain't no Barlow," I said. "I'm Breckinridge Elkins, of Bear Creek. I ain't never even heard of no Barlows."

At that Jim stopped his groaning long enough to snarl: "If you ain't a friend of the Barlows, how come you askin' for Dick Jackson? He's one of 'em."

"He jilted my sister!" I roared. "I aim to drag him back and make him marry her!"

"Well, it was all a mistake," groaned Jim. "But the damage is done now."

"It's wuss'n you think," said the gal fiercely. "The Hopkinses has all forted theirselves over at pap's cabin, and they sent me to git you all. We got to make a stand. The Barlows is gatherin' over to Jake Barlow's cabin, and they aims to make a foray onto us tonight. We was outnumbered to begin with, and now here's our best fightin' men laid out! Our goose is cooked plumb to hell!"

"Lift me on my horse," moaned Jim. "I can't walk, but I can still shoot." He tried to rise up, and fell back cussing and groaning.

"You got to help us!" said the gal desperately, turning to me. "You done laid out our four best fightin' men, and you owes it to us. It's yore duty! Anyway, you says Dick Jackson's yore enemy—well, he's Jake Barlow's nephew, and he come back here to help 'em clean out us Hopkinses. He's over to Jake's cabin right now. My brother Bill snuck over and spied on 'em, and he says every fightin' man of the clan is gatherin' there. All we can do is hold the fort, and you got to come help us hold it! Yo're nigh as big as all four of these boys put together."

Well, I figgered I owed the Hopkinses something, so, after setting some bones and bandaging some wounds and abrasions of which they was a goodly lot, I saddled Cap'n Kidd and we sot out.

As we rode along she said: "That there is the biggest, wildest, meanest-lookin' critter I ever seen. Where'd you git him?"

"He was a wild horse," I said. "I catched him up in the Humbolts. Nobody ever rode him but me. He's the only horse west of the Pecos big enough to carry my weight, and he's got painter's blood and a shark's disposition. What's this here feud about?"

"I dunno," she said. "It's been goin' on so long everybody's done forgot what started it. Somebody accused somebody else of stealin' a cow, I think. What's the difference?"

"They ain't none," I assured her. "If folks wants to have feuds its their own business."

We was following a winding path, and purty soon we heard dogs barking and about that time the gal turned aside and got off her horse, and showed me a pen hid in the brush. It was full of horses.

"We keep our mounts here so's the Barlows ain't so likely to find 'em and run 'em off," she said, and she turned her horse into the pen, and I put Cap'n Kidd in, but tied him over in one corner by hisself — otherwise he would of started fighting all the other horses and kicked the fence down.

Then we went on along the path and the dogs barked louder and purty soon we come to a big two-story cabin which had heavy board-shutters over the winders. They was just a dim streak of candle light come through the cracks. It was dark, because the moon hadn't come up. We stopped in the shadder of the trees, and the gal whistled like a whippoorwill three times, and somebody answered from up on the roof. A door opened a crack in the room which didn't have no light at all, and somebody said: "That you, Elizerbeth? Air the boys with you?"

"It's me," says she, starting toward the door. "But the boys ain't with me."

Then all to once he throwed open the door and hollered: "Run, gal! They's a grizzly b'ar standin' up on his hind laigs right behind you!"

"Aw, that ain't no b'ar," says she. "That there's Breckinridge Elkins, from up in Nevady. He's goin' to help us fight the Barlows."

WE WENT ON INTO A ROOM where they was a candle on the table, and they was nine or ten men there and thirty-odd women and chillern. They all looked kinda pale and scairt, and the men was loaded down with pistols and Winchesters.

They all looked at me kind of dumb-like, and the old man kept staring like he warn't any too sure he hadn't let a grizzly in the house, after all. He mumbled something about making a natural mistake, in the dark, and turned to the gal.

"Whar's the boys I sent you after?" he demanded, and she says: "This gent mussed 'em up so's they ain't fitten for to fight. Now, don't git rambunctious, pap. It war just a honest mistake all around. He's our friend, and he's gunnin' for Dick Jackson."

"Ha! Dick Jackson!" snarled one of the men, lifting his Winchester. "Just lemme line my sights on him! I'll cook his goose!"

"You won't, neither," I said. "He's got to go back to Bear Creek and marry my sister Ellen.... Well," I says, "what's the campaign?"

"I don't figger they'll git here till well after midnight," said Old Man Hopkins. "All we can do is wait for 'em."

"You means you all sets here and waits till they comes and lays siege?" I says.

"What else?" says he. "Lissen here, young man, don't start tellin' me how to conduck a feud. I growed up in this here'n. It war in full swing when I was born, and I done spent my whole life carryin' it on."

"That's just it," I snorted. "You lets these dern wars drag on for generations. Up in the Humbolts we brings such things to a quick conclusion. Mighty near everybody up there come from Texas, original, and we fights our feuds Texas style, which is short and sweet—a feud which lasts ten years in Texas is a humdinger. We winds 'em up quick and in style. Where-at is this here cabin where the Barlow's is gatherin'?"

"'Bout three mile over the ridge," says a young feller they called Bill.

"How many is they?" I ast.

"I counted seventeen," says he.

"Just a fair-sized mouthful for a Elkins," I said. "Bill, you guide me to that there cabin. The rest of you can come or stay, it don't make no difference to me."

Well, they started jawing with each other then. Some was for going and some for staying. Some wanted to go with me and try to take the Barlows by surprise, but the others said it couldn't be done—they'd git ambushed theirselves, and the only sensible thing to be did was to stay forted and wait for the Barlows to come. They given me no more heed—just sot there and augered.

But that was all right with me. Right in the middle of the dispute, when it looked like maybe the Hopkinses' would get to fighting amongst theirselves and finish each other before the Barlows could git there, I lit out with the boy Bill, which seemed to have considerable sense for a Hopkins.

He got him a horse out of the hidden corral, and I got Cap'n Kidd, which was a good thing. He'd somehow got a mule by the neck, and the critter was almost at its last gasp when I rescued it. Then me and Bill lit out.

We follered winding paths over thick-timbered mountainsides till at last we come to a clearing and they was a cabin there, with light and profanity pouring out of the winders. We'd been hearing the last mentioned for half a mile before we sighted the cabin.

We left our horses back in the woods a ways, and snuck up on foot and stopped amongst the trees back of the cabin.

"They're in there tankin' up on corn licker to whet their appetites for Hopkins blood!" whispered Bill, all in a shiver. "Lissen to 'em! Them fellers ain't hardly human! What you goin' to do? They got a man standin' guard out in front of the door at the other end of the cabin. You see they ain't no doors nor winders at the back. They's winders on each side, but if we try to rush it from the front or either side, they'll see us and fill us full of lead before we could git in a shot. Look! The moon's comin' up. They'll be startin' on their raid before long."

I'll admit that cabin looked like it was going to be harder to storm than I'd figgered. I hadn't had no idee in mind when I sot out for the place. All I wanted was to get in amongst them Barlows—I does my best fighting at close quarters. But at the moment I couldn't think of no way that wouldn't get me shot up. Of course I could just rush the cabin, but the thought of seventeen Winchesters blazing away at me from close range was a little stiff even for me, though I was game to try it, if they warn't no other way.

Whilst I was studying over the matter, all to once the horses tied out in front of the cabin snorted, and back up the hills something went *Oooaaaw-w-w!* And a idee hit me.

"Git back in the woods and wait for me," I told Bill, as I headed for the thicket where we'd left the horses.

I MOUNTED AND RODE up in the hills toward where the howl had come from. Purty soon I lit and throwed Cap'n Kidd's reins over his head, and walked on into the deep bresh, from time to time giving a long squall like a cougar. They ain't a catamount in the world can tell the difference when a Bear Creek man imitates one. After a while one answered, from a ledge just a few hundred feet away.

I went to the ledge and clumb up on it, and there was a small cave behind it, and a big mountain lion in there. He give a grunt of surprize when he seen I was a human, and made a swipe at me, but I give him a bat on the head with my fist, and whilst he was still dizzy I grabbed him by the scruff of the neck and hauled him out of the cave and lugged him down to where I left my horse.

Cap'n Kidd snorted at the sight of the cougar and wanted to kick his brains out, but I give him a good kick in the stummick hisself, which is the only kind of reasoning Cap'n Kidd understands, and got on him and headed for the Barlow hangout.

I can think of a lot more pleasant jobs than toting a full-growed mountain lion down a thick-timbered mountain side on the back of a iron jaw outlaw at midnight. I had the cat by the back of the neck with one hand, so hard he couldn't squall, and I held him out at arm's length as far from the horse as I could, but every now and then he'd twist around so he could claw Cap'n Kidd with his hind laigs, and when this would happen Cap'n Kidd would squall with rage and start bucking all over the place. Sometimes he would buck the derned cougar onto me, and pulling him loose from my hide was wuss'n pulling cockle-burrs out of a cow's tail.

But presently I arriv close behind the cabin. I whistled like a whippoorwill for Bill, but he didn't answer and warn't nowheres to be seen, so I decided he'd got scairt and pulled out for home. But that was all right with me. I'd come to fight the Barlows, and I aimed to fight 'em, with or without assistance. Bill would just of been in the way.

I got off in the trees back of the cabin and throwed the reins over Cap'n Kidd's head, and went up to the back of the cabin on foot, walking soft and easy. The moon was well up, by now, and what wind they was, was blowing toward me, which pleased me, because I didn't want the horses tied out in front to scent the cat and start cutting up before I was ready.

The fellers inside was still cussing and talking loud as I approached one of the winders on the side, and one hollered out: "Come on! Let's git started! I craves Hopkins gore!" And about that time I give the cougar a heave and throwed him through the winder.

He let out a awful squall as he hit, and the fellers in the cabin hollered louder'n he did. Instantly a most awful bustle broke loose in there and of all the whooping and bellering and shooting I ever heard, and the lion squalling amongst it all, and clothes and hides tearing so you could hear it all over the clearing, and the horses busting loose and tearing out through the bresh.

As soon as I hove the cat I run around to the door and a man was standing there with his mouth open, too surprised at the racket to do anything. So I takes his rifle away from him and broke the stock off on his head, and stood there at the door with the barrel intending to brain them Barlows as they run out. I was plumb certain they *would* run out, because I have noticed that the average man is funny that way, and hates to be shut up in a cabin with a mad cougar as bad as the cougar would hate to be shut up in a cabin with a infuriated settler of Bear Creek.

But them scoundrels fooled me. 'Pears like they had a secret door in the back wall, and whilst I was waiting for them to storm out through the front door and get their skulls cracked, they knocked the secret door open and went piling out that way.

BY THE TIME I REALIZED what was happening and run around to the other end of the cabin, they was all out and streaking for the trees, yelling blue murder, with their clothes all tore to shreds and them bleeding like stuck hawgs.

That there catamount sure improved the shining hours whilst he was corralled with them Barlows. He come out after 'em with his mouth full of the seats of men's britches, and when he seen me he give a kind of despairing yelp and taken out up the mountain with his tail betwixt his laigs like the devil was after him with a red-hot branding iron.

I taken after the Barlows, sot on scuttling at least a few of 'em, and I was on the p'int of letting *bam* at 'em with my six-shooters as they run, when, just as they reached the trees, all the Hopkins men riz out of the bresh and fell on 'em with piercing howls.

That fray was kind of peculiar. I don't remember a single shot being fired. The Barlows had dropped their guns in their flight, and the Hopkinses seemed bent on whipping out their wrongs with their bare hands and gun butts. For a few seconds they was a hell of a scramble—men cussing and howling and bellering, and rifle-stocks cracking over heads, and the bresh crashing underfoot, and then before I could get into it, the Barlows broke every which-way and took out through the woods like jack-rabbits squalling Jedgment Day.

Old Man Hopkins come prancing out of the bresh waving his Winchester and his beard flying in the moonlight and he hollered: "The sins of the wicked shall return onto 'em! Elkins, we have hit a powerful lick for righteousness this here night!"

"Where'd you all come from?" I ast. "I thought you was still back in yore cabin chawin' the rag."

"Well," he says, "after you pulled out we decided to trail along and see how you come out with whatever you planned. As we come through the woods expectin' to git ambushed every second, we met Bill here who told us he believed you had a idee of circumventin' them devils, though he didn't know what it was. So we come on and hid ourselves at the aidge of the trees to see what'd happen. I see we been too timid in our dealin's with these heathens. We been lettin' them force the fightin' too long. You was right. A good offense is the best defense.

"We didn't kill any of the varmints, wuss luck," he said, "but we give 'em a prime lickin'. Hey, look there! The boys has caught one of the critters! Take him into that cabin, boys!"

They lugged him into the cabin, and by the time me and the old man got there, they had the candles lit, and a rope around the Barlow's neck and one end throwed over a rafter.

That cabin was a sight, all littered with broke guns and splintered chairs and tables, pieces of clothes and strips of hide. It looked just about like a cabin ought to look where they has just been a fight between seventeen polecats and a mountain lion. It was a dirt floor, and some of the poles which helped hold up the roof was splintered, so most of the weight was resting on a big post in the center of the hut.

All the Hopkinses was crowding around their prisoner, and when I looked over their shoulders and seen the feller's pale face in the light of the candle I give a yell: "Dick Jackson!"

"So it is!" said Old Man Hopkins, rubbing his hands with glee. "So it is! Well, young feller, you got any last words to orate?"

"Naw," said Jackson sullenly. "But if it hadn't been for that derned lion spilin' our plans we'd of had you danged Hopkinses like so much pork. I never heard of a cougar jumpin' through a winder before."

"That there cougar didn't jump," I said, shouldering through the mob. "He was hev. I done the heavin'."

His mouth fell open and he looked at me like he'd saw the ghost of Sitting Bull. "Breckinridge Elkins!" says he. "I'm cooked now, for sure!"

"I'll say you air!" gritted the feller who'd spoke of shooting Jackson earlier in the night. "What we waitin' for? Le's string him up."

The rest started howlin'.

"Hold on," I said. "You all can't hang him. I'm goin' to take him back to Bear Creek."

"You ain't neither," said Old Man Hopkins. "We're much obleeged to you for the help you've give us tonight, but this here is the first chance we've had to hang a Barlow in fifteen year, and we aim to make the most of it. String him, boys!"

"Stop!" I roared, stepping for'ard.

IN A SECOND I WAS COVERED by seven rifles, whilst three men laid hold of the rope and started to heave Jackson's feet off the floor. Them seven Winchesters didn't stop me. But for one thing I'd of taken them guns away and wiped up the floor with them ungrateful mavericks. But I was afeared Jackson would get hit in the wild shooting that was certain to foller such a plan of action.

What I wanted to do was something which would put 'em all horse-de-combat as the French say, without killing Jackson. So I laid hold on the center-post and before they knowed what I was doing, I tore it loose and broke it off, and the roof caved in and the walls fell inwards on the roof.

In a second they wasn't no cabin at all—just a pile of lumber with the Hopkinses all underneath and screaming blue murder. Of course I just braced my laigs and when the roof fell my head busted a hole through it, and the logs of the falling walls hit my shoulders and glanced off, so when the dust settled I was standing waist-deep amongst the ruins and nothing but a few scratches to show for it.

The howls that riz from beneath the ruins was blood-curdling, but I knowed nobody was hurt permanent because if they was they wouldn't be able to howl like that. But I expect some of 'em would of been hurt if my head and shoulders hadn't kind of broke the fall of the roof and wall-logs.

I located Jackson by his voice, and pulled pieces of roof board and logs off until I come onto his laig, and I pulled him out by it and laid him on the ground to get his wind back, because a beam had fell acrost his stummick and when he tried to holler he made the funniest noise I ever heard.

I then kind of rooted around amongst the debris and hauled Old Man Hopkins out, and he seemed kind of dazed and kept talking about earthquakes.

"You better git to work extricatin' yore misguided kin from under them logs, you hoary-haired old sarpent," I told him sternly. "After that there display of ingratitude I got no sympathy for you. In fact, if I was a short-tempered man I'd feel inclined to violence. But bein' the soul of kindness and generosity, I controls my emotions and merely remarks that if I *wasn't* mild-mannered as a lamb, I'd hand you a boot in the pants—like this!"

I kicked him gentle.

"Owww!" says he, sailing through the air and sticking his nose to the hilt in the dirt. "I'll have the law on you, you derned murderer!" He wept, shaking his fists at me, and as I departed with my captive I could hear him chanting a hymn of hate as he pulled chunks of logs off of his bellering relatives.

Jackson was trying to say something, but I told him I warn't in no mood for perlite conversation and the less he said the less likely I was to lose my temper and tie his neck into a knot around a black jack.

CAP'N KIDD MADE THE hundred miles from the Mezquital Mountains to Bear Creek by noon the next day, carrying double, and never stopping to eat, sleep, nor drink. Them that don't believe that kindly keep their mouths shet. I have already licked nineteen men for acting like they didn't believe it.

I stalked into the cabin and throwed Dick Jackson down on the floor before Ellen which looked at him and me like she thought I was crazy.

"What you finds attractive about this coyote," I said bitterly, "is beyond the grasp of my dust-coated brain. But here he is, and you can marry him right away."

She said: "Air you drunk or sun-struck? Marry that good-for-nothin', whiskey-swiggin', card-shootin' loafer? Why, ain't been a week since I run him out of the house with a buggy whip."

"Then he didn't jilt you?" I gasped.

"Him jilt me?" she said. "I jilted him!"

I turned to Dick Jackson more in sorrer than in anger.

"Why," said I, "did you boast all over Chawed Ear about jiltin' Ellen Elkins?"

"I didn't want folks to know she turned me down," he said sulkily. "Us Jacksons is proud. The only reason I ever thought about marryin' her was I was ready to settle down, on the farm pap gave me, and I wanted to marry me a Elkins gal so I wouldn't have to go to the expense of hirin' a couple of hands and buyin' a span of mules and—"

They ain't no use in Dick Jackson threatening to have the law on me. He got off light to what's he'd have got if pap and my brothers hadn't all been off hunting. They've got terrible tempers. But I was always too soft-hearted for my own good. In spite of Dick Jackson's insults I held my temper. I didn't do nothing to him at all, except escort him in sorrow for five or six miles down the Chawed Ear trail, kicking the seat of his britches.

THE END

The Haunted Mountain

The reason I despises tarantulas, stinging lizards, and hydrophobia skunks is because they reminds me so much of Aunt Lavaca, which my Uncle Jacob Grimes married in a absent-minded moment, when he was old enough to know better.

That-there woman's voice plumb puts my teeth on aidge, and it has the same effect on my horse, Cap'n Kidd, which don't generally shy at nothing less'n a rattlesnake. So when she stuck her head out of her cabin as I was riding by and yelled "Breckinri-i-idge," Cap'n Kidd jumped straight up in the air, and then tried to buck me off.

"Stop tormentin' that pore animal and come here," Aunt Lavaca commanded, whilst I was fighting for my life against Cap'n Kidd's spine-twisting sun-fishing. "I never see such a cruel, worthless, no-good—"

She kept right on yapping away until I finally wore him down and reined up alongside the cabin stoop and said: "What you want, Aunt Lavaca?"

She give me a scornful snort, and put her hands onto her hips and glared at me like I was something she didn't like the smell of.

"I want you should go git yore Uncle Jacob and bring him home," she said at last. "He's off on one of his idiotic prospectin' sprees again. He snuck out before daylight with the bay mare and a pack mule—I wisht I'd woke up and caught him. I'd of fixed him! If you hustle you can catch him this side of Haunted Mountain Gap. You bring him back if you have to lasso him and tie him to his saddle. Old fool! Off huntin' gold when they's work to be did in the alfalfa fields. Says he ain't no farmer. Huh! I 'low I'll make a farmer outa him yet. You git goin'."

"But I ain't got time to go chasin' Uncle Jacob all over Haunted Mountain," I protested. "I'm headin' for the rodeo over to Chawed Ear. I'm goin' to win me a prize bull-doggin' some steers—"

"Bull-doggin'!" she snapped. "A fine ockerpashun! Gwan, you worthless loafer! I ain't goin' to stand here all day argyin' with a big ninny like you be. Of all the good-for-nothin', triflin', lunkheaded—"

When Aunt Lavaca starts in like that you might as well travel. She can talk steady for three days and nights without repeating herself, her voice getting louder and shriller all the time till it nigh splits a body's eardrums. She was still yelling at me as I rode up the trail toward Haunted Mountain Gap, and I could hear her long after I couldn't see her no more.

Pore Uncle Jacob! He never had much luck prospecting, but trailing around through the mountains with a jackass is a lot better'n listening to Aunt Lavaca. A jackass's voice is mild and soothing alongside of hers.

Some hours later I was climbing the long rise that led up to the Gap, and I realized I had overtook the old coot when something went *ping!* up on the slope, and my hat flew off. I quick reined Cap'n Kidd behind a clump of bresh, and looked up toward the Gap, and seen a packmule's rear-end sticking out of a cluster of boulders.

"You quit that shootin' at me, Uncle Jacob!" I roared.

"You stay whar you be," his voice come back, sharp as a razor. "I know Lavacky sent you after me, but I ain't goin' home. I'm onto somethin' big at last, and I don't aim to be interfered with."

"What you mean?" I demanded.

"Keep back or I'll ventilate you," he promised. "I'm goin' for the Lost Haunted Mine."

"You been huntin' that thing for thirty years," I snorted.

"This time I finds it," he says. "I bought a map off'n a drunk Mex down to Perdition. One of his ancestors was a Injun which helped pile up the rocks to hide the mouth of the cave where it is."

"Why didn't he go find it and git the gold?" I asked.

"He's skeered of ghosts," said Uncle Jacob. "All Mexes is awful superstitious. This-un 'ud ruther set and drink, nohow. They's millions in gold in that-there mine. I'll shoot you before I'll go home. Now will you go on back peaceable, or will you throw-in with me? I might need you, in case the pack mule plays out."

"I'll come with you," I said, impressed. "Maybe you have got somethin', at that. Put up yore Winchester. I'm comin'."

He emerged from his rocks, a skinny leathery old cuss, and he said: "What about Lavacky? If you don't come back with me, she'll foller us herself. She's that strong-minded."

"I'll leave a note for her," I said. "Joe Hopkins always comes down through the Gap onct a week on his way to Chawed Ear. He's due through here today. I'll stick the note on a tree, where he'll see it and take it to her."

I had a pencil-stub in my saddle-bag, and I tore a piece of wrapping paper off'n a can of tomaters Uncle Jacob had in his pack, and I writ:

Dere Ant Lavaca:

I am takin uncle Jacob way up in the mountins dont try to foler us it wont do no good gold is what Im after. Breckinridge.

I folded it and writ on the outside:

Dere Joe: pleeze take this here note to Miz Lavaca Grimes on the Chawed Ear rode.

THEN ME AND UNCLE JACOB sot out for the higher ranges, and he started telling me all about the Lost Haunted Mine again, like he'd already did about forty times before. Seems like they was onct a old prospector which stumbled onto a cave about fifty years before then, which the walls was solid gold and nuggets all over the floor till a body couldn't walk, as big as mushmelons. But the Indians jumped him and run him out and he got lost and nearly starved in the desert, and went crazy. When he come to a settlement and finally regained his mind, he tried to lead a party back to it, but never could find it. Uncle Jacob said the Indians had took rocks and bresh and hid the mouth of the cave so nobody could tell it was there. I asked him how he knowed the Indians done that, and he said it was common knowledge. Any fool oughta know that's just what they done.

"This-here mine," says Uncle Jacob, "is located in a hidden valley which lies away up amongst the high ranges. I ain't never seen it, and I thought I'd explored these mountains plenty. Ain't nobody more familiar with 'em than me except old Joshua Braxton. But it stands to reason that the cave is awful hard to find, or somebody'd already found it. Accordin' to this-here map, that lost valley must lie just beyond Apache Canyon. Ain't many white men knows whar that is, even. We're headin' there."

We had left the Gap far behind us, and was moving along the slanting side of a sharp-angled crag whilst he was talking. As we passed it, we seen two figgers with horses emerge from the other side, heading in the same direction we was, so our trails converged. Uncle Jacob glared and reached for his Winchester.

"Who's that?" he snarled.

"The big un's Bill Glanton," I said. "I never seen t'other'n."

"And nobody else, outside of a freak museum," growled Uncle Jacob.

This other feller was a funny-looking little maverick, with laced boots and a cork sun-helmet and big spectacles. He sot his horse like he thought it was a rocking chair, and held his reins like he was trying to fish with 'em. Glanton hailed us. He was from Texas, original, and was rough in his speech and free with his weapons, but me and him had always got along very well.

"Where you-all goin'?" demanded Uncle Jacob.

"I am Professor Van Brock, of New York," said the tenderfoot, whilst Bill was getting rid of his tobaccer wad. "I have employed Mr. Glanton, here, to guide me up into the mountains. I am on the track of a tribe of aborigines, which, according to fairly well substantiated rumor, have inhabited the Haunted Mountains since time immemorial."

"Lissen here, you four-eyed runt," said Uncle Jacob in wrath, "are you givin' me the horse-laugh?"

"I assure you that equine levity is the furthest thing from my thoughts," says Van Brock. "Whilst touring the country in the interests of science, I heard the rumors to which I have referred. In a village possessing the singular appellation of Chawed Ear, I met an aged prospector who told me that he had seen one of the aborigines, clad in the skin of a wild animal and armed with a bludgeon. The wildman, he said, emitted a most peculiar and piercing cry when sighted, and fled into the recesses of the hills. I am confident that it is some survivor of a pre-Indian race, and I am determined to investigate."

"They ain't no such critter in these hills," snorted Uncle Jacob. "I've roamed all over 'em for thirty year, and I ain't seen no wildman."

"Well," says Glanton, "they's *somethin'* onnatural up there, because I been hearin' some funny yarns myself. I never thought I'd be huntin' wildmen," he says, "but since that hash-slinger in Perdition turned me down to elope with a travelin' salesman, I welcomes the chance to lose myself in the mountains and forget the perfidy of women-kind. What you-all doin' up here? Prospectin'?" he said, glancing at the tools on the mule.

"Not in earnest," said Uncle Jacob hurriedly. "We're just kinda whilin' away our time. They ain't no gold in these mountains."

"Folks says that Lost Haunted Mine is up here somewhere," said Glanton.

"A pack of lies," snorted Uncle Jacob, busting into a sweat. "Ain't no such mine. Well, Breckinridge, let's be shovin'. Got to make Antelope Peak before sundown."

"I thought we was goin' to Apache Canyon," I says, and he give me a awful glare, and said: "Yes, Breckinridge, that's right, Antelope Peak, just like you said. So long, gents."

"So long," said Glanton.

So we turned off the trail almost at right-angles to our course, me follerin' Uncle Jacob bewilderedly. When we was out of sight of the others, he reined around again.

"When Nature give you the body of a giant, Breckinridge," he said, "she plumb forgot to give you any brains to go along with yore muscles. You want everybody to know what we're lookin' for?"

"Aw," I said, "them fellers is just lookin' for wildmen."

"Wildmen!" he snorted. "They don't have to go no further'n Chawed Ear on payday night to find more wildmen than they could handle. I ain't swallerin' no such stuff. Gold is what they're after, I tell you. I seen Glanton talkin' to that Mex in Perdition the day I bought that map from him. I believe they either got wind of that mine, or know I got that map, or both."

"What you goin' to do?" I asked him.

"Head for Apache Canyon by another trail," he said.

SO WE DONE SO AND ARRIV there after night, him not willing to stop till we got there. It was deep, with big high cliffs cut with ravines and gulches here and there, and very wild in appearance. We didn't descend into the canyon that night, but camped on a plateau above it. Uncle Jacob 'lowed we'd begin exploring next morning. He said they was lots of caves in the canyon, and he'd been in all of 'em. He said he hadn't never found nothing except b'ars and painters and rattlesnakes; but he believed one of them caves went on through into another, hidden canyon, and there was where the gold was at.

Next morning I was awoke by Uncle Jacob shaking me, and his whiskers was curling with rage.

"What's the matter?" I demanded, setting up and pulling my guns.

"They're here!" he squalled. "Daw-gone it, I suspected 'em all the time! Git up, you big lunk. Don't set there gawpin' with a gun in each hand like a idjit! They're here, I tell you!"

"Who's here?" I asked.

"That dern tenderfoot and his cussed Texas gunfighter," snarled Uncle Jacob. "I was up just at daylight, and purty soon I seen a wisp of smoke curlin' up from behind a big rock t'other side of the flat. I snuck over there, and there was Glanton fryin' bacon, and Van Brock was pertendin' to be lookin' at some flowers with a magnifyin' glass—the blame fake. He ain't no perfessor. I bet he's a derned crook. They're follerin' us. They aim to murder us and rob us of my map."

"Aw, Glanton wouldn't do that," I said. And Uncle Jacob said: "You shet up! A man will do anything whar gold is consarned. Dang it all, git up and do somethin'! Air you goin' to set there, you big lummox, and let us git murdered in our sleep?"

That's the trouble of being the biggest man in yore clan; the rest of the family always dumps all the onpleasant jobs onto yore shoulders. I pulled on my boots and headed across the flat, with Uncle Jacob's war-songs ringing in my ears, and I didn't notice whether he was bringing up the rear with his Winchester or not.

They was a scattering of trees on the flat, and about halfway across a figger emerged from amongst them, headed my direction with fire in his eye. It was Glanton.

"So, you big mountain grizzly," he greeted me rambunctiously, "you was goin' to Antelope Peak, hey? Kinda got off the road, didn't you? Oh, we're on to you, we are!"

"What you mean?" I demanded. He was acting like he was the one which oughta feel righteously indignant, instead of me.

"You know what I mean!" he says, frothing slightly at the mouth. "I didn't believe it when Van Brock first said he suspicioned you, even though you hombres did act funny yesterday when we met you on the trail. But this mornin' when I glimpsed yore fool Uncle Jacob spyin' on our camp, and then seen him sneakin' off through the bresh, I knowed Van Brock was right. Yo're after what we're after, and you-all resorts to dirty onderhanded tactics. Does you deny yo're after the same thing we are?"

"Naw, I don't," I said. "Uncle Jacob's got more right to it than you-all. And when you says we uses underhanded tricks, yo're a liar."

"That settles it!" gnashed he. "Go for yore gun!"

"I don't want to perforate you," I growled.

"I ain't hankerin' to conclude yore mortal career," he admitted. "But Haunted Mountain ain't big enough for both of us. Take off yore guns and I'll maul the livin' daylights outa you, big as you be."

I unbuckled my gun-belt and hung it on a limb, and he laid off his'n, and hit me in the stummick and on the ear and in the nose, and then he socked me in the jaw and knocked out a tooth. This made me mad, so I taken him by the neck and throwed him against the ground so hard it jolted all the wind outa him. I then sot on him and started banging his head against a convenient boulder, and his cussing was terrible to hear.

"If you all had acted like white men," I gritted, "we'd of *give* you a share in that there mine."

"What you talkin' about?" he gurgled, trying to haul his bowie out of his boot which I had my knee on.

"The Lost Haunted Mine, of course," I snarled, getting a fresh grip on his ears.

"Hold on," he protested. "You mean you-all are just lookin' for gold? On the level?"

I was so astonished I quit hammering his skull against the rock.

"Why, what else?" I demanded. "Ain't you-all follerin' us to steal Uncle Jacob's map which shows where at the mine is hid?"

"Git offa me," he snorted disgustfully, taking advantage of my surprize to push me off. "Hell!" he said, starting to knock the dust offa his britches. "I might of knowed that tenderfoot was wool-gatherin'. After we seen you-all yesterday, and he heard you mention 'Apache Canyon' he told me he believed you was follerin' us. He said that yarn about prospectin' was just a blind. He said he believed you was workin' for a rival scientific society to git ahead of us and capture that-there wildman yoreselves."

"What?" I said. "You mean that wildman yarn is straight?"

"So far as we're consarned," said Bill. "Prospectors is been tellin' some onusual stories about Apache Canyon. Well, I laughed at him

27

at first, but he kept on usin' so many .45-caliber words that he got me to believin' it might be so. 'Cause, after all, here was me guidin' a tenderfoot on the trail of a wildman, and they wasn't no reason to think you and Jacob Grimes was any more sensible than me.

"Then, this mornin' when I seen Joab peekin' at me from the bresh, I decided Van Brock must be right. You-all hadn't never went to Antelope Peak. The more I thought it over, the more sartain I was that you was follerin' us to steal our wildman, so I started over to have a showdown."

"Well," I said, "we've reached a understandin' at last. You don't want our mine, and we shore don't want yore wildman. They's plenty of them amongst my relatives on Bear Creek. Le's git Van Brock and lug him over to our camp and explain things to him and my weak-minded uncle."

"All right," said Glanton, buckling on his guns. "Hey, what's that?"

From down in the canyon come a yell: "Help! Aid! Assistance!"

"It's Van Brock!" yelped Glanton. "He's wandered down into the canyon by hisself! Come on!"

RIGHT NEAR THEIR CAMP they was a ravine leading down to the floor of the canyon. We pelted down that at full speed, and emerged near the wall of the cliffs. They was the black mouth of a cave showing nearby, in a kind of cleft, and just outside this cleft Van Brock was staggering around, yowling like a hound dawg with his tail caught in the door.

His cork helmet was laying on the ground all bashed outa shape, and his specs was lying near it. He had a knob on his head as big as a turnip and he was doing a kind of ghost-dance or something all over the place.

He couldn't see very good without his specs, 'cause when he sighted us he give a shriek and starting legging it for the other end of the canyon, seeming to think we was more enemies. Not wanting to indulge in no sprint in that heat, Bill shot a heel offa his boot, and that brung him down squalling blue murder.

"Help!" he shrieked. "Mr. Glanton! Help! I am being attacked! Help!"

"Aw, shet up," snorted Bill. "I'm Glanton. Yo're all right. Give him his specs, Breck. Now what's the matter?"

He put 'em on, gasping for breath, and staggered up, wild-eyed, and p'inted at the cave and hollered: "The wildman! I saw him, as I descended into the canyon on a private exploring expedition! A giant with a panther-skin about his waist, and a club in his hand. He dealt me a murderous blow with the bludgeon when I sought to apprehend him, and fled into that cavern. He should be arrested!"

I looked into the cave. It was too dark to see anything except for a hoot-owl.

"He must of saw *somethin'*, Breck," said Glanton, hitching his gun-harness. "Somethin' shore cracked him on the conk. I've been hearin' some queer tales about this canyon, myself. Maybe I better sling some lead in there—"

"No, no, no!" broke in Van Brock. "We must capture him alive!"

"What's goin' on here?" said a voice, and we turned to see Uncle Jacob approaching with his Winchester in his hands.

"Everything's all right, Uncle Jacob," I said. "They don't want yore mine. They're after the wildman, like they said, and we got him cornered in that there cave."

"All right, huh?" he snorted. "I reckon you thinks it's all right for you to waste yore time with such dern foolishness when you oughta be helpin' me look for my mine. A big help you be!"

"Where was you whilst I was argyin' with Bill here?" I demanded.

"I knowed you could handle the sityation, so I started explorin' the canyon," he said. "Come on, we got work to do."

"But the wildman!" cried Van Brock. "Your nephew would be invaluable in securing the specimen. Think of science! Think of progress! Think of—"

"Think of a striped skunk!" snorted Uncle Jacob. "Breckinridge, air you comin'?"

"Aw, shet up," I said disgustedly. "You both make me tired. I'm goin' in there and run that wildman out, and Bill, you shoot him in the hind-laig as he comes out, so's we can catch him and tie him up."

"But you left yore guns hangin' onto that limb up on the plateau," objected Glanton.

"I don't need 'em," I said. "Didn't you hear Van Brock say we was to catch him alive? If I started shootin' in the dark I might rooin him."

"All right," says Bill, cocking his six-shooters. "Go ahead. I figger yo're a match for any wildman that ever come down the pike."

So I went into the cleft and entered the cave, and it was dark as all get-out. I groped my way along and discovered the main tunnel split into two, so I taken the biggest one. It seemed to get darker the further I went, and purty soon I bumped into something big and hairy and it went "Wump!" and grabbed me.

Thinks I, it's the wildman, and he's on the war-path. We waded into each other and tumbled around on the rocky floor in the dark, biting and mauling and tearing. I'm the biggest and the fightingest man on Bear Creek, which is famed far and wide for its ring-tailed scrappers, but this wildman shore give me my hands full. He was the biggest hairiest critter I ever laid hands on, and be had more teeth and talons than I thought a human could possibly have. He chawed me with

30

vigor and enthusiasm, and he waltzed up and down my frame free and hearty, and swept the floor with me till I was groggy.

For a while I thought I was going to give up the ghost, and I thought with despair of how humiliated my relatives on Bear Creek would be to hear their champion battler had been clawed to death by a wildman in a cave.

That made me plumb ashamed for weakening, and the socks I give him ought to of laid out any man, wild or tame, to say nothing of the pile-driver kicks in his belly, and butting him with my head so he gasped. I got what felt like a ear in my mouth and commenced chawing on it, and presently, what with this and other mayhem I committed on him, he give a most inhuman squall and bust away and went lickety-split for the outside world.

I riz up and staggered after him, hearing a wild chorus of yells break forth outside, but no shots. I bust out into the open, bloody all over, and my clothes hanging in tatters.

"Where is he?" I hollered. "Did you let him git away?"

"Who?" said Glanton, coming out from behind a boulder, whilst Van Brock and Uncle Jacob dropped down out of a tree nearby.

"The wildman, damn it!" I roared.

"We ain't seen no wildman," said Glanton.

"Well, what was that thing I just run outa the cave?" I hollered.

"That was a grizzly b'ar," said Glanton. "Yeah," sneered Uncle Jacob, "and that was Van Brock's 'wildman'! And now, Breckinridge, if yo're through playin', we'll—"

"No, no!" hollered Van Brock, jumping up and down. "It was a human being which smote me and fled into the cavern. Not a bear! It is still in there somewhere, unless there is another exit to the cavern."

31

"Well, he ain't in there now," said Uncle Jacob, peering into the mouth of the cave. "Not even a wildman would run into a grizzly's cave, or if he did, he wouldn't stay long—ooomp!"

A rock come whizzing out of the cave and hit Uncle Jacob in the belly, and he doubled up on the ground.

"Aha!" I roared, knocking up Glanton's ready six-shooter. "I know! They's two tunnels in here. He's in that smaller cave. I went into the wrong one! Stay here, you-all, and gimme room! This time I gets him!"

WITH THAT I RUSHED INTO the cave mouth again, disregarding some more rocks which emerged, and plunged into the smaller opening. It was dark as pitch, but I seemed to be running along a narrer tunnel, and ahead of me I heered bare feet pattering on the rock. I follered 'em at full lope, and presently seen a faint hint of light. The next minute I rounded a turn and come out into a wide place, which was lit by a shaft of light coming in through a cleft in the wall, some yards up. In the light I seen a fantastic figger climbing up on a ledge, trying to reach that cleft.

"Come down offa that!" I thundered, and give a leap and grabbed the ledge by one hand and hung on, and reached for his legs with t'other hand. He give a squall as I grabbed his ankle and splintered his club over my head. The force of the lick broke off the lip of the rock ledge I was holding to, and we crashed to the floor together, because I didn't let loose of him. Fortunately, I hit the rock floor headfirst which broke my fall and kept me from fracturing any of my important limbs, and his head hit my jaw, which rendered him unconscious.

I riz up and picked up my limp captive and carried him out into the daylight where the others was waiting. I dumped him on the ground and they stared at him like they couldn't believe it. He was a ga'nt old cuss with whiskers about a foot long and matted hair, and he had a mountain lion's hide tied around his waist.

"A white man!" enthused Van Brock, dancing up and down. "An unmistakable Caucasian! This is stupendous! A prehistoric survivor of a pre-Indian epoch! What an aid to anthropology! A wildman! A veritable wildman!"

"Wildman, hell!" snorted Uncle Jacob. "That-there's old Joshua Braxton, which was tryin' to marry that old maid schoolteacher down at Chawed Ear all last winter."

"*I* was tryin' to marry her!" said Joshua bitterly, setting up suddenly and glaring at all of us. "That-there is good, that-there is! And me all the time fightin' for my life against it. Her and all her relations was tryin' to marry *her* to me. They made my life a curse. They was finally all set to kidnap me and marry me by force. That's why I come away off up here, and put on this rig to scare folks away. All I craves is peace and quiet and no dern women."

Van Brock begun to cry because they wasn't no wildman, and Uncle Jacob said: "Well, now that this dern foolishness is settled, maybe I can git to somethin' important. Joshua, you know these mountains even better'n I do. I want you to help me find the Lost Haunted Mine."

"There ain't no such mine," said Joshua. "That old prospector imagined all that stuff whilst he was wanderin' around over the desert crazy."

"But I got a map I bought from a Mexican in Perdition," hollered Uncle Jacob.

"Lemme see that map," said Glanton. "Why, hell," he said, "that-there is a fake. I seen that Mexican drawin' it, and he said he was goin' to try to sell it to some old jassack for the price of a drunk."

Uncle Jacob sot down on a rock and pulled his whiskers. "My dreams is bust," he said weakly. "I'm goin' home to my wife."

"You must be desperate if it's come to that," said old Joshua acidly. "You better stay up here. If they ain't no gold, they ain't no women to torment a body, either."

"Women is a snare and a delusion," agreed Glanton. "Van Brock can go back with these fellers. I'm stayin' with Joshua."

"You-all oughta be ashamed talkin' about women that way," I reproached 'em. "What, in this here lousy and troubled world can compare to women's gentle sweetness—"

"There the scoundred is!" screeched a familiar voice. "Don't let him git away! Shoot him if he tries to run!"

WE TURNED SUDDEN. We'd been argying so loud amongst ourselves we hadn't noticed a gang of folks coming down the ravine. There was Aunt Lavaca and the sheriff of Chawed Ear with ten men, and they all p'inted sawed-off shotguns at me.

"Don't get rough, Elkins," warned the sheriff nervously. "They're all loaded with buckshot and ten-penny nails. I knows yore repertation and I takes no chances. I arrests you for the kidnapin' of Jacob Grimes."

"Are you plumb crazy?" I demanded.

"Kidnapin'!" hollered Aunt Lavaca, waving a piece of paper. "Abductin' yore pore old uncle! Aimin' to hold him for ransom! It's all writ down in yore own handwritin' right here on this-here paper! Sayin' yo're takin' Jacob away off into the mountains—warnin' me not to try to foller! Same as threatenin' me! I never heered of such doin's! Soon as that good-for-nothin' Joe Hopkins brung me that there insolent letter, I went right after the sheriff.... Joshua Braxton, what *air* you doin' in them ondecent togs? My land, I dunno what we're comin' to! Well, sheriff, what you standin' there for like a ninny? Why'n't you put some handcuffs and chains and shackles on him? Air you skeered of the big lunkhead?"

"Aw, heck," I said. "This is all a mistake. I warn't threatenin' nobody in that there letter—"

"Then where's Jacob?" she demanded. "Prejuice him imejitately, or—"

"He ducked into that cave," said Glanton.

I stuck my head in and roared: "Uncle Jacob! You come outa there and explain before I come in after you!"

He snuck out looking meek and down-trodden, and I says: "You tell these idjits that I ain't no kidnaper."

"That's right," he said. "I brung him along with me."

"Hell!" said the sheriff, disgustedly. "Have we come all this way on a wild goose chase? I should of knew better'n to listen to a woman"

"You shet yore fool mouth!" squalled Aunt Lavaca. "A fine sheriff you be. Anyway—what was Breckinridge doin' up here with you, Jacob?"

"He was helpin' me look for a mine, Lavacky," he said.

"Helpin' you?" she screeched. "Why, I sent him to fetch you back! Breckinridge Elkins, I'll tell yore pap about this, you big, lazy, good-for-nothin', low-down, ornery—"

"Aw, shet up!" I roared, exasperated beyond endurance. I seldom lets my voice go its full blast. Echoes rolled through the canyon like thunder, the trees shook and the pine cones fell like hail, and rocks tumbled down the mountainsides. Aunt Lavaca staggered backwards with a outraged squall.

"Jacob!" she hollered. "Air you goin' to 'low that ruffian to use that-there tone of voice to me? I demands that you flail the livin' daylights outa the scoundrel right now!"

Uncle Jacob winked at me.

"Now, now, Lavacky," he started soothing her, and she give him a clip under the ear that changed ends with him. The sheriff and his posse and Van Brock took out up the ravine like the devil was after 'em, and Glanton bit off a chaw of tobaccer and says to me, he says: "Well, what was you fixin' to say about women's gentle sweetness?"

"Nothin'," I snarled. "Come on, let's git goin'. I yearns to find a more quiet and secluded spot than this-here'n. I'm stayin' with Joshua and you and the grizzly."

THE END